How to Negotiate EVERYTHING

DAVID SPELLMAN
WITH LISA LUTZ

ILLUSTRATED BY
JAIME TEMAIRIK

Simon & Schuster Books for Young Readers

NEW YORK   LONDON   TORONTO   SYDNEY   NEW DELHI

To Stephanie Kip Rostan
—L. L.

To Rae Spellman
—D. S.

To Lisa Lutz
—J. T.

ACKNOWLEDGMENTS

Special thanks to everyone at Simon & Schuster—
especially Justin Chanda, Laurent Linn, and Julia Maguire.

—L. L. & J. T.

SIMON & SCHUSTER BOOKS FOR YOUNG READERS • An imprint of Simon & Schuster Children's Publishing Division • 1230 Avenue of the Americas, New York, New York 10020 • Text copyright © 2012 by Lisa Lutz • Illustrations copyright © 2012, 2013 by Jaime Temairik • Text and portions of illustrations has been previously published in 2012 in *Trail of the Spellmans*. • All rights reserved, including the right of reproduction in whole or in part in any form. • SIMON & SCHUSTER BOOKS FOR YOUNG READERS is a trademark of Simon & Schuster, Inc. • For information about special discounts for bulk purchases, please contact Simon & Schuster Special Sales at 1-866-506-1949 or business@simonandschuster. com. • The Simon & Schuster Speakers Bureau can bring authors to your live event. For more information or to book an event, contact the Simon & Schuster Speakers Bureau at 1-866-248-3049 or visit our website at www.simonspeakers.com. • Book design by Laurent Linn • The text for this book is set in Syntax LT Std. • The illustrations for this book are rendered digitally. • Manufactured in China • 0313 SCP • 10 9 8 7 6 5 4 3 2 1 • Library of Congress Cataloging-in-Publication Data • Spellman, David. • How to negotiate everything / David Spellman with Lisa Lutz ; illustrated by Jaime Temairik. • p. cm. • ISBN 978-1-4424-5119-3 (hardcover) • ISBN 978-1-4424-5120-9 (eBook) • 1. Negotiation— Juvenile literature. I. Lutz, Lisa. II. Title. • BF637.N4S66 2012 • 302.3—dc23 • 2011038386

first edition

Have you ever wanted something and **didn't get it?**

Have you ever **begged**, **cried**, or **screamed** for a special toy or an ice-cream cone or a visit to the zoo or a puppy or a turtle or a pair of sneakers with flashing lights?

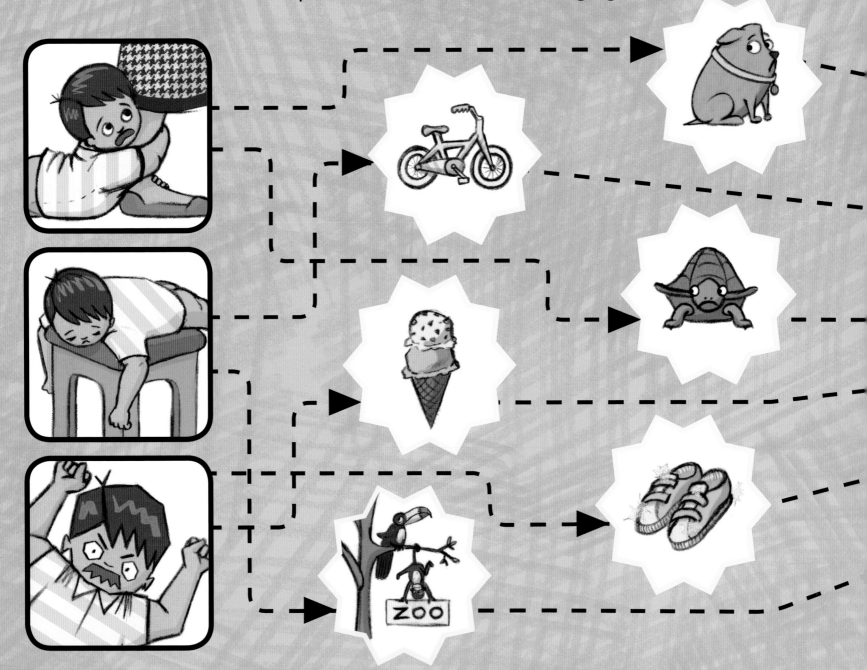

Is the answer **always** . . .

We feel your pain.

The truth is, we often don't get what we want
and then we let our emotions take over.

But **CRYING** is **NOT** the answer.

Can I let you in on a little secret?

You **CAN** get everything you want.

Stop crying for a few minutes and I'll tell you how it's done.

BE RATIONAL

Do you know what RATIONAL means?
Rational is when you can remain calm and
thoughtful and use your words, not your emotions.

There are very few things in life that you can't get if you ask for them in a rational manner and offer something in return. That's called "**negotiating**."

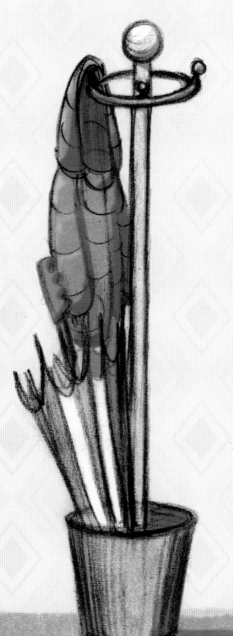

Let's see how Sammy negotiates with his mother. . . .

At the beginning of a negotiation always be polite.

Now Sammy must ask himself, **can he wait for the ice cream?**

He probably can.

MANAGING EXPECTATIONS

Remember when we said that there are very few things you can't get if you ask for them in a rational manner?

Sammy had made a good deal, but he thought he could do better. However, you have to be sure you can get what you are asking for. Then you won't be disappointed.

Sometimes you can negotiate *too* aggressively.

Let's take a look at how negotiations can go **wrong**.

OVERREACHING

Sammy let his successful ice-cream negotiation go to his head.
When he was in the market for a new pet, he contemplated his options.

But none of those ordinary pets would do.
Sammy thought long and hard about what
he really wanted and he asked for it.

Sammy negotiated **aggressively**.

He offered to eat broccoli **for an entire year**.

He promised to clean his room and make his bed **every day**.

He vowed to **stop** calling his little sister Dork Face.

But Sammy's mom was like a brick wall.
She wouldn't budge.
Her answer was a flat-out

And Sammy eventually settled for **a turtle**.

It's a sad fact, but some things
in life are **non-negotiable**.

NOT SURE YOUR NEGOTIATION GOAL IS *REALISTIC*?

Here's a quick guide:

Shoes

Small pets

Cotton candy

WORTH NEGOTIATING FOR

(You just might get what you want!)

Trips to the zoo

More television time

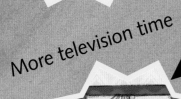

Trips to other places where you look at things

A wombat

Real estate (that means houses or large parcels of land)

A motorcycle

NOT WORTH NEGOTIATING FOR

Endangered species

Quitting school and joining the circus

A diet consisting entirely of candy

And remember the most important part of negotiating . . .

BE PERSISTENT

When you grow up, you can take negotiating to a new level.
Remember that elephant Sammy wanted? Well, it wasn't just a passing fancy.

He still wanted it.

People told him that having a pet elephant was an impossible dream.
But Sammy didn't listen to them.
All he had to do was **negotiate**.

Items that once seemed impossible to acquire
will **now** be at your fingertips.

GLOSSARY

Aggressive: Ask for more than you think you might get. When Sammy asked for an elephant, he was negotiating aggressively.

In the bag: A cool way to say that things are going your way.

Long-term strategy: You may not win your negotiation right away. In that case, look into the future, like Sammy did, and come up with a plan.

Mark: Your mark is the person you are negotiating with. When Sammy wanted ice cream, his mark was his mother.

Negotiate: You should know what this word means by now.

Persistent: Staying focused. Pursuing your goal no matter how impossible it seems. When people say "no" to Sammy, he hears "maybe."

Rational: This is the magic word in negotiating. When Sammy stopped throwing tantrums to get what he wanted and began negotiating, he was being rational.

Settling: Sometimes you won't get everything you want in a negotiation. At first Sammy settled for a turtle when he asked for an elephant.

Weakness: Everybody wants something, and that desire makes it easier to negotiate with your mark. Find out what your mark's weakness is (quiet, candy, wine, elephants) and you've got your negotiation in the bag.

DON'T BE A RAT:
primer on how to use snitch-worthy
material to your advantage.

THAT'S ENOUGH OUT OF YOU:
How to silence a chatterbox and get
on with your day

YOU'RE NOT THE BOSS OF ME:
How to outwit the babysitter

POWER SHOWERS AND PEANUTS
How to care for your pet elephant